D1530267

CAM & the BiG, MEAN duck

Written by Kathleen Rouse   Illustrated by Miles Davis

Dear Ms. Collier,

Thank you for the opportunity to send "Cam and the Big Mean Duck" to you for consideration! This Teacher's Guide is meant to give you some ideas to continue children's learning after they read the story of "Cam and the Big Mean Duck".

I hope you enjoy the book! If you are looking for authors to read during online book readings I would be happy to read to the group and share this guide.

Sincerely,

Kathleen Rouse

Teacher's Guide

Name the feeling:

Cam experiences a lot of different feelings throughout the book.

Name the feeling Cam experiences:

1. Cam wakes up and her mom shows her it is time to feed the ducks
2. Cam gets to the park and starts to feed the ducks
3. Cam sees the big mean duck steal all the food
4. Cam sees the other ducks are sad when the big mean duck steals their food
5. Cam notices the big mean duck is sad when he can't get up to eat the sweet duck treats of grapes
6. Cam and the big mean duck talk when the duck realizes it feels better to share

Draw your feelings:

Now that you named the different feelings Cam experienced, draw pictures of when you felt those feelings before.

Draw your own duck:

The big mean duck is big and white, draw your own duck. Is your duck mean like the one in the book or is it nice? What color is your duck? What does your duck like to do?

How many?

Count the ducks in the book. How many do you see?
Count the trees in the book. How many and what shapes are the trees?

What do you like to do at the park?

What do you like to do at the park with your family?
Draw a picture of your perfect day at the park.
Do you like to feed the ducks? Do you like to go on the swings?   Do you like to look at the flowers or trees?

CAM & the BiG MEAN Duck

Written by Kathleen Rouse   Illustrated by Miles Davis

DORRANCE
PUBLISHING CO
EST. 1920
PITTSBURGH, PENNSYLVANIA 15238

Dorrance Publishing Co
585 Alpha Drive
Pittsburgh, PA 15238
Visit our website at *www.dorrancebookstore.com*

ISBN: 978-1-4809-8609-1
eISBN: 978-1-4809-8591-9

To Lucy & Manny who filled my childhood with good memories.

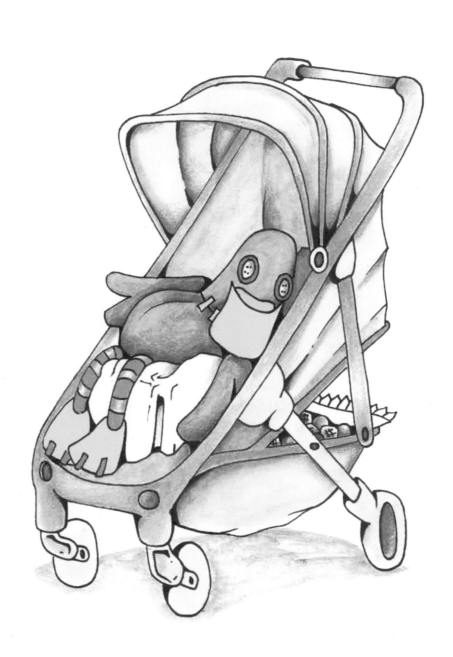

Cam is awake; It's not too late

To feed the ducks on the lake.

Cam's stroller is packed with loving care –
Let's get out and enjoy the fresh air!

Cam's head in a hat, looking so sweet;

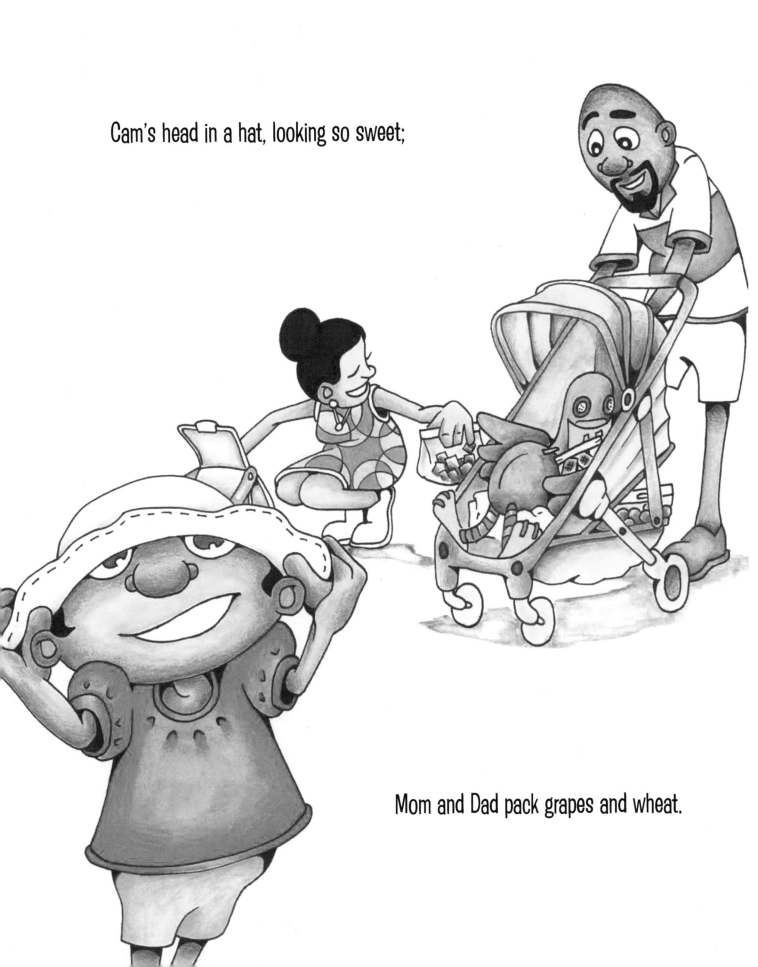

Mom and Dad pack grapes and wheat.

Cam giggles with a clap
As ducks swim and quack.

But, a big, mean duck comes with wings-a-flap.

He grabs the wheat and makes Cam mad!

He swims away; the other ducks are sad.

The big, mean duck flaps his wings with a sway.
And takes from the others along the way.

Cam tosses more food, trying to brighten the mood.
The other ducks are frightened, so they just brood.

Duck's belly is too full. He can't move his feet.
Then Cam pulls out the grapes, a sweet duck treat!

The others quack and happily eat
As he looks on in defeat.

Cam sees he's sad and says,
"Here you go, Duck!"

He looks up with a surprised cluck.

Cam tosses a taste.
It won't go to waste.

All the ducks are happily eating.
One does a dance, his wings joyfully beating.

No longer so mean, the duck swims back;
He finds Cam and lets out a grateful quack!

"Thanks!" he says to Cam.
"Without question, I've learned my lesson.
It feels good to care. Now, I will share."

Dad scoops Cam up. The visit comes to an end.

She waves goodbye to the duck. "You're welcome, my friend."